# Sunny Side Up

Mehwish Fatima, Riddhima Sen

**Ukiyoto Publishing**

*We would like express our heartfelt gratitude to Ukiyoto Publishing House for providing us with valuable opportunity.*

# Contents

# Take Your Time And Think

Take your time think about what you want to do go through everything and just start your day the focus needs to be maintained the goal needs to be strong and the only thing left is to achieve it work upon it don't just step out back run and run on path at one time it's not easy to achieve it but the time will come when it is going to be achieved and make feel so happy that the hard work has turned into success that success will give smile on everyone's face and is going to be so great for reaching on heights it will take time it will not happen suddenly but slowly – slowly things will change lots of hurdles come to stop but they will go away if one keep on running on the same path the hurdles will get tierd and want to go  lots and lots of things may come to distract the focus but on time they will also go back only the diligency and hardwork will stay back there and take to the golden path of success.

# Don't Leave A Person Lone Make Them Feel Happy

Lonliness makes a person sad and brings up a feeling of staying alone the happiness blow away the fun goes somewhere and the person starts staying in some uneasy state which is not good for health it's something which makes a person weak and the thoughts goes round and round which gathers and pack the persons mind it does not go easily it stays for longer, it shouts in mind and become bigger and captures the whole mind.

Cheer up and gear up the person who feels like and make them out of that so they could again smile and feel confident about everything which goes on and on in mind cheer up with full concentration and bring the person out of the situation gear up so that they can again enjoy the life and can stay happily with full fun the life is to live with happiness and together not lonely and conciously because lonliness does not make person happy but make person lone.

# Enjoy Each Day Beacuse It's Your Own

Enjoy each and everyday with fun make your day a very special one because ecah day begins with freshness and happiness each day reminds new and old memories just feel the beginning and ending of dawn to dusk.

Any be something going to special happen something very interesting is coming or something going to be joyous which makes mind happier and calm all the tension will go away and a new beginning will be instilled.

Spend each day with positivity and not negativity each day is so wonderful and so important it teaches many things the management of time, how to maintain routine,how to work from time to time and many more.

Each day is going to be memorious enjoy with full happiness band cheerfulness do all work with calm mind and get succeed in your goal and achieve something big don't loose hope just utilise each day with some works.

# They Are Tears

I asked them that why sometimes you are do u controllable that you all come on your own why are you all so unstoppable that when one wipes you then also you come why won't you all stop after a second you all take minutes to stop the one feels so sad and can't able to stop the one feels to sit somewhere and hide the face all lonliness comes to mind you all also feel sad and come out you are also in pain and the person too.

They answered that they come out of eyes suddenly when someone hurts or when someone talks rudely they said they are sometimes uncontrollable because the person is in deep hurt they couldn't able to stop they flow and flow they are in paint too and see the persons pain they swiftly takes place in one's eye and start coming out the one feels so unhappy that hides the face and then cry we also cry on seeing the one hurt badly.

They are tears who has narrated their story that what happens that suddenly they come how it affects them how the one gets sad and hide the face and start to cry and sometimes the person hide form everyone and alone somewhere calls the tears the tears too feel the pain of one crying and crying how the one is feeling so uneasy from inside and just calling out tears to come they are tears who feel sad for everyone.

# You Are Confident and You Can Do It

Just imagine yourself standing alone in forest and speaking there loud that you are confident and can do it never feel low just keep your spirit don't be afraid or scared just speak up then only the fear will go away.

Tell your stage fear to go away stand infront of mirror and speak by seeing yourself speak and speak make yourself strong and confident then try to speak infront of everyone then see the magic of yourself.

Don't back out just go for it and prove yourself that you are also winner if you think that you can't then you can't but if you think that you can then you can don't loose hope just fill all positivity inside yourself.

Slowly and slowly your confidence will start getting instilled and the feeling of being confident comes in don't think negative think all positive don't loose chance just go for it once it goes then it can't return again so be ready for it.

Take all challenges and speak for it just go for it mark it as important and give up your best think of giving best infront of the whole people watching who are cheering and the people who are clapping don't miss the golden chance.

Speak and speak it's your time do the best of it and then see the big change in yourself which will bring a big smile on face and that smile is very special what If not won the participation is the first step to be a winner next time.

# Feelings

Some feelings are so good but some feelings make emotional and sad the feelings comes on their own upon listening something or upon hearing something feelings to are uncontrollable they just come on their own the happy feeling make feels so special but there the unhappy feeling makes one feel sad not only sad but the one starts to think about it on their own.

It touches the heart happy feeling makes some very special space for happiness but some feeling closes the space of happiness the one feels low and disturbed about some feeling there are some which builds up the strength but there are some which pulls down the strength but what to do only the thing is to fight from the unhappy feeling and wake up the happiest feeling in mind and heart.

They slowly become close and make the mind depends on their state feelings become important for the one they become very special and sometimes they become doubtful the one feels good for someone and sometimes the one thinks feelings depend on person when they come they are sudden they do not tell anybody anything they just come they make relax but at time they make u happy.

Feelings you are very different you come so swiftly and go in some time you make mind relax but sometime you hesitate mind when you come our mind depends on you that of what nature you are of good or bad one feelings come in a good mood and make mind calm give rest to mind,feelings give happiness and make mind full of joy that when someone feel you they can relax their mind.

# Encourage Yourself and Others Don't Discourage

Encourage yourself in each and every task encourage yourself in every work that you do or the work given to you go ahead and just do it there you will disbalance but you will surely balance yourself and that makes you feel more stronger encourage yourself don't discourage

Don't feel sad and don't feel low try to keep yourself calm sit plan in your mind what further to do and if you feel that you can't never discourage yourself just encourage yourself and move on the path that you are moving don't move backward move straight on the path.

Look straight bring your head up don't put it down encourage yourself and slowly start taking your head up if you put it down there will be only sadness no smile don't bring sadness just try to gear up yourself for work for studies and for every situation that you will be going to face.

No don't turn back otherwise you won't succeed face it remove the barriers by your strength and just walk and walk don't think everything is closed nothing is left it's your thought nothing has been closed everything has just opened now the time has come to face it and go for it.

Don't listen to the one who are discouraging straight up yourself and feels that you are alone and look forward a golden door of opportunities is waiting there for you it's standing only the thing is just take up the key and open the door there you could see the world of tasks don't give up.

Negative thoughts say no to them instill postive thoughts they are going to work with you don't discourage yourself with negative thoughts your mind will get disturbed take a deep breathe and call all positivity in yourself make yourself happy with what you are going to achieve after taking the opportunity.

Never get down always work hard to bring up yourself and focus on the opportunity that you have got think of that and try to achieve something great if you loose the opportunity you will feel unhappy and that unhappiness will affect many of your closed ones and they too will feel the unhappiness of yours.

So make an aim that whenever the time of taking up an opportunity of completing the task don't run back run straight forward take it up with confidence and complete it encourage yourself don't discourage if you discourage yourself you could not be able to achieve anything.

Take your decision because it is very important what do you think while taking decisions the right decision don't discourage yourself and don't take tough decision take the right one in which everything is going to be fine and will work one wrong decision can tell you to just give up and step back

All the best for your work do it well and stand up well in your work prove yourself that you are an encouraging person and you have encouraged yourself and got the result which has made you more and more stronger prove that you have not discouraged yourself and has always moved towards right direction.

With encouraging yourself encourage others also if they are not getting any solution of the problem they are facing don't let them discourage themselves make them also strong give them the positivity that you have instilled of doing and taking up the opportunity of completing the task or in any situation.

Face each and every situation by encouraging yourself and encouraging other to face the situation don't discourage if you discourage you will feel low which will not work don't let the other also get discouraged they will also think that they have not succeeded strengthen up your power and the other's also.

Once you will get the habit of encouraging then you won't be able to stop yourself you will with encouraging other's will succeed in your way and will be going to achieve big no negative thoughts will distract you only postive thoughts will build up in mind which will lead to greater heights.

# Just Imagine And Feel The Change

Are you getting tired and not getting anything to do go draw something or listen good music and enjoy have fun write something interesting take your diary pick up your pen and start writing about something fun about a journey on hills or about a dream or what you want to become and what all things you want to do if you don't want to write or listen music then imagine.

Imagine that you are on hills just imagine it's beauty there are birds singing song there are trees blooming with full joy they are so green the atmosphere is so cool you are walking and walking between the trees you can listen the sound of the waterfall the flowers are too enjoying with the pleasant weather the blue sky and with the golden light the sun is shining.

Just imagine the sun is setting down slowly- slowly and the sunset seen is so nice the birds are going home the night comes up the stars are shining up on the sky the moon is giving light to walk on the road the weather becomes more cool everyone is going home after their work the bazaars are filled with people everyone is buying something and laughing and talking everyone is happy.

Just imagine your success journey see yourself working hard and practicing and trying to do your best and you have become so strong and said that I will do and will never step back I can do and will try to prove myself by my focus and by my confidence think and think that you can cross all the hurdles and will go ahead the hurdles are disturbing you and you will say them not to disturb.

When you close your eyes that relaxed feeling makes you comfartable and you can calm down your mind by imagining which will make you feel happy and then you can perfectly focus on the work that you want to do keep your self happy and imagine whenever you feel bored or don't want to write or listen music imagine yourself the fun with your family and friends and then you will feel happy and calm.

# Don't Take Stress

Don't take stress just calm down yourself make a timetable for your work and then start preparing for it don't just mix everything up maybe you will get confused take rest and then sit for study don't get hesitated by seeing too many things to read and learn plan up one by one how to start with and what to start first then start learning and write in your notebook and then see you can learn it.

Slowly start learning and then make it little fast and learn and learn once it gets learned note it down try to recall in your free time watch something knowledgeable take a break, listen to good music to keep yourself out of stress, eat something healthy and then start again never loose up your hope just do it you will feel happy understand the chapter line by line and then learn it you will get it.

Just try to make your mind think that you can do it and you can work upon it tell yourself that you can score up good and can do it don't step out back just work hard and hard ignore the things that are disturbing you and focus on your studies just focus once you will give full attention to it all your disturbing things will go away and you can do it always think positive and good and go ahead.

# Tell Your Stage Fear To Go Away

Why are you getting afraid go speak up and perform on stage you can do it and can do it very well don't get sacred or think that you can't do you can do it don't feel nervous make yourself relaxed and comfartable and perform think and think that you can do well and going to bring your talent up show up your talent of performing and then see your result that you have preformed very nicely the claps and cheers are waiting for you to prove up yourself just close your eyes and think that you are alone standing in the hall nobody is there when there you can do then you can perform infront of many people just go for it and showcase the hidden talent of yourself think that you are best and you have prepared well for that and then try to do it think that you have learnt it by hard and then go for it just think that when you complete up the claps and cheers who are waiting just start up and the noise should go higher and higher think and think and just perform you can do it tell your stage fear to go away.

# Be Happy Because Your Happiness Is Important

Be happy because your happiness is important if you stay sad always then your loved ones will feel sad for you try to encourage yourself and stay happy don't think too much think slowly – slowly  try to make yourself comfartable and relaxed try to calm down your mind don't hesitate don't panic don't make yourself stressed try to be happy and smile.

If you will stay happy then your loved ones will also stay happy seeing you share your problems with them so that you will feel relaxed and they too try to understand what has made you so sad whenever you feel sad start working upon something complete up your work or go out to play keep yourself in some work so you will feel happy and not sad that much.

Be happy because your happiness is important if you stay sad always then your loved ones will feel sad for you, you are so special for your family for your friends whenever you feel sad they get to know about it just go to them and share up your things don't keep that in yourself otherwise the stress will make you weak and you then don't want to do anything try to keep yourself happy.

# Don't Loose Hope

Don't loose hope, hope that you will win and you are a winner and you will keep up this going on, be confident, be strong don't let your strength go down just keep it up just think about your success and proceed then see that you can do it you are a winner and you can win it don't get afraid just tell your fear to go away don't think too much that your interest will go away just think about the topic and gather information on it and present yourself and then see your confidence will show up that how better you can do.

Don't loose hope, hope that you will win and you are a winner don't hide your inner talent just show up yourself you have lots of talent hidden inside you and you can do it once you think you can't do at the second attempt you think that now also your base is not strong but at the third attempt you will surely succeed don't think that you are not confident always think that you are confident, don't think that you are weak no you are not weak, don't think that your base is not strong your base is strong,don't loose hope.

# You Are Beautiful You Are Pretty

You are so beautiful, you are pretty  don't think that you are not thank God for making you, you are very talented and you are very intelligent don't think you are not always think you are just cheer up for yourself and go ahead always think good about yourself and don't think wrong you are best, you are wonderful, you have all good qualities and can go further just see yourself and speak that you are beautiful and you are good.

Motivate up yourself don't demotivate just show up your talents think all well just feel the good things and don't feel wrong just cheer up for yourself you will always stay good don't feel down just keep up yourself just see the beauty that has hidden in you and show it up think and think and think about your happiness not your sadness think up about yourself you are beautiful you are pretty thank god for making you, you are very talented.

# Don't Step Back Go Ahead

No, no, no don't step out back don't tgo back move ahead, move ahead you have to face it you have to do it just close your eyes and go ahead don't leave it take up the opportunity you ah e to prove up yourself you have to make it realise everyone that you can do it and you can raise up the claps  and cheers for yourself the door is waiting  for you to come and knock it so that it is going to open up for you many of the people are waiting for you to come and meet them and you have to go don't feel that you can't do make up your mind and go for it you have to handle it and you have to move ahead so that you can easily solve and get all your solutions just go ahead and take up the opportunity.

# Hurdles Are Tough But You Have To Cross It

Hurdles are very tough to cross they are easy sometimes, hard and ok that yes can cross it but many of the times it's very tough but what to do we have to cross it to reach the door the golden door of the challenges the opportunity that is waiting for you don't have to move back and don't get afraid that you can't do you can do and have to do it you have to cross the hurdles because you have to achieve your goal focus on your aim and just go ahead imagine that it's easy you have to work hard for it and reach it you have to reach the heights and prove up yourself you don't have to move back you have to move front once you think in your mind that you have to do something good and reach to the door you will surely reach it and do great you can cross hurdles and you will cross the hurdles and you will reach the door of success.

# The Kaleidoscope of calamity

Numerous flints of fire,

Bright orange and yellow,

Humongous boulders rolling down the mountain tops,

Streaked with tints of dark brown and hot red lava;

Erupting from the volcanous peaks of Krakatoa,

In August 1883.


The devastating cry of the innocent infants,

Holding on to their mother's arms,

Petrified beyond apprehension,

Young naïve teenagers;

And young women clad in lavender garments,

With floral prints embroidered on them,

Zillions of innocent people

Who fell prey to a natural calamity?

And died within a microsecond.

# The Shades Of Insanity

How can we describe insanity?

Maybe a   condition of   mental instability,

Where a person is retarded mentally

Devoid of the capacity to think normally

But,

Is that really the definition of insanity?


The hustles and bustles of daily life

Filled with excessive workload,

Hypertension,

And a pile of deadlines

And assignments and files

Isn't that insanity?

Of modern issues

And lifestyle?

# Anguish

Tones of anguish,
Filled with numerous voids
Dyed with hues of anguish
Dark grey tigered with specks of black;
Spread across the horizon.

What is anguish?
A severe state of depression;
An abyss of sheer darkness
Hemmed in by the beautiful elements of nature
As dark as Hade's kingdom,
Grim and dormant.

# What Is Eavesdropping?

Maybe secretly listening to someone's conversation,

But what does it really signify:

To a child's amateur mind,

It's like delving deep into the world of maturity

Infested with complex mundanitites

Accompanied by dismal truths of life,

Unveiled and exposed.

# Conversation

Lily:   Hey, Cactus, how are you doing?

Cactus:  Hey, I'm good. What about you?

Lily:  Yeah, I am hale and hearty as ever, what can even go wrong with me when I'm so white and pure.  You are so rough and unsophisticated.

Cactus:  I am not ugly, your thoughts are ugly and filthy.

# The Red Letter

Bloody footprints of puberty,

Left on the spotless sanitary napkins;

As white as the pure innocent souls

Of naïve, young maidens

Standing on the threshold of maturity

And immaturity,

Still not clear on how to develop into a mature woman,

Once the caterpillar exposes itself from the pupae

It explores the world around itself

Which is enthralling,

Yet abound in dangers.

The journey from maidenhood to womanhood is quite tricky,

An unpredictable journey;

Full of breakups, heartaches, harassment, and bullying

An emotionally jarring rollercoaster ride

Which is a quintessential part of a woman's life

A path worth embarking upon.

# **Journal Entry**

Wonderful, lustrous garments
Woven with numerous colourful threads,
Tints of bright scarlet,
Mountain blue, the representative of tranquillity;
And pastel shades, subtle yet pretty.

# Anecdotes Of Scribbling

December 2014: Dry, shrunken leaves

Trapped among the white pages,

Of the bright blue velvet diary,

Intertwined with numerous memories;

Of the winter fall

Of the valuable days spent at the yellow school building,

Oh, the vivid memories of playing tic-tac-toe,

And the fresh smell of the woollen sweaters,

Memoirs of the golden, old days.


May, 2015:   Finally, the much-awaited wait has come to an end,

Fully grown birds will fly away afar,

Farther from the comfortable nest

And the amiable environment of their second homes;

It's a rather painful separation,

As if the bosom is being extracted from the human body,

A bag of skeletons and muscles,

Bidding a teary and jittery adieu to twelve years of nostalgia,

Is an amalgamation of exuberance and pensive, gloomy thoughts, surely?

# Hues Of Mundanity

Colourful hues beaming through the horizon,
Eloquent tints of turquoise blue;
Tigered with shades of baby pink,
And tinged with hues of exuberance,
Spread all across the hues mundanity,
These are the hues of mundanity,
The insignia of daily activities,
Abounding in sorrow,   yet
The smell of coffee emerging from the ceramic table,
The much acquainted fabric of the cotton t-shirts
With words   that motivate
Are mundane yet precious.

Shrivelled petals of roses,
Strewn all along the path,
Chrome yellow with the dust of life,
Coated with mendacity,
Monotonous shades of dull grey
Tinted with speckles of black
Which represent life,

In its rawest self;
Embledded in darkening shapes
Leaning against the sidewalk
Life is just a rollercoaster ride, truly.

# Faded Dandelions

My love, do you still remember
The days of explicit bliss;
When we were companions,
Bosom companions who could never be separated.
Lovers for an eternal timespan,

I still remember,
The warm smell of your blue cotton t-shirt,
The comfortable space in the lawn
Where we used to talk our hearts out,
Now, you have abandoned me
We may never be united again,
But, the memory of the sultry evening
Clinging to the fabric of your nylon cardigan
My pink sweater,

Continues to be persistent
Down my memory lane
The elegant view of the cherry blossoms
Strewn in my heart,
Light pinkish speckles
On my bleeding heart,
People go away,

But memories remain.

Although my heartstrings are baked with blood,
And embellished with the innards of my faint heart
I still cherish the memories of La Amour.
The dandelions have faded, beloved.

# Liberty

What is liberty?
A feeling of freedom,
Immense, unlimited
Just like the azure sky
Wide and immeasurable.

# Hues Of Disturbance

Oh, those hues of sadness,
Frilled with iced peaks,
Icicles,
All black and blue,
And;
Streaks of dull grey
Flaming across the sky

# Vrai Soi

What is our true self?

Maybe a depiction of our internal psyche

An amalgamation of id, ego and superego,

Irrepressible urges,

Pangs of exuberance, libido, and lust.

# Pearls Of Silence

On a dreary day,
Long and pensive;
After a hard day at the office,
Slogging in an air-conditioned room
Silence is like a word spoken easily

Silent words and silent days,
Falling off the sky like pearls from an oyster
Composed of clouds and sediments.
Baby pink and dark grey,
With speckles of gold.
And heart-warming motivation.

# The Vessel Of Life

Man : What is the meaning of life?

Philosopher : Well, it's an individual's journey from the starting point to the ending point.

Man : If life is so miserable,  and full of challenges,  why should we live it ?

Philosopher: Because the vessel of life crosses the river of faith, compassion, kindness and positivity atleast once, it does not always face tempestuous winds which cause the seas to shriek, and emit salty tears in the form of waves. The vessel of life is crafted with rosewood and  redwood, at the same time. It's a journey worth embarking upon, even though it's an amalgamation of happiness and sadness.

www.ingramcontent.com/pod-product-compliance
Lightning Source LLC
LaVergne TN
LVHW041443170726
843492LV00008B/2782